Dollar General Literacy Grant

PATRICIA POLACCO

Uncle Vova's TREE

PUFFIN BOOKS

With love to my friend in Leningrad,
Margarita Alexandrova Ivanova.

PUFFIN BOOKS

Published by the Penguin Group

Penguin Young Readers Group, 345 Hudson Street, New York, New York 10014, U.S.A.

Penguin Group (Canada), 90 Eglinton Avenue East, Suite 700, Toronto, Ontario, Canada M4P 2Y3 (a division of Pearson Penguin Canada Inc.)

Penguin Books Ltd, 80 Strand, London WC2R 0RL, England

Penguin Ireland, 25 St Stephen's Green, Dublin 2, Ireland (a division of Penguin Books Ltd)

Penguin Group (Australia), 250 Camberwell Road, Camberwell, Victoria 3124, Australia (a division of Pearson Australia Group Pty Ltd)

Penguin Books India Pvt Ltd, 11 Community Centre, Panchsheel Park, New Delhi - 110 017, India

Penguin Group (NZ), 67 Apollo Drive, Rosedale, North Shore 0632, New Zealand (a division of Pearson New Zealand Ltd)

Penguin Books (South Africa) (Pty) Ltd, 24 Sturdee Avenue, Rosebank, Johannesburg 2196, South Africa

Registered Offices: Penguin Books Ltd, 80 Strand, London WC2R 0RL, England

First published in the United States of America by Philomel Books, a division of Penguin Putnam Books for Young Readers, 1989
Published by Puffin Books, a division of Penguin Young Readers Group, 2009

1 3 5 7 9 10 8 6 4 2

Text and illustrations copyright © Patricia Polacco, 1989
All rights reserved

THE LIBRARY OF CONGRESS HAS CATALOGED THE PHILOMEL BOOKS EDITION AS FOLLOWS:
Polacco, Patricia.
Uncle Vova's tree / Patricia Polacco.
p. cm.
Summary: Grandparents, aunts and uncles, and children gather at a farm house to celebrate Christmas in the Russian tradition.
ISBN: 0-399-21617-0 (hc)
[1. Christmas—Fiction. 2. Russian Americans—Fiction.] I. Title.
PZ7.P75186Un 1989 [Fic]—dc19 88-25522 CIP AC

Puffin Books ISBN 978-0-14-241483-5

Manufactured in China

Book design by Nanette Stevenson

During the Russian Orthodox calendar year, no holiday is more loved than Christmastide and Epiphany. As a child I celebrated Christmas as most American children did, but at Epiphany in January, my brother, my two cousins, my grandparents and I would go to the farm of my Great Uncle Vladimir and Aunt Svetlana to celebrate in the Russian tradition. We wore dress from the homeland and relived the customs that originated from my family's roots. There is a wonder and a kind of magic that arises out of such dear memories. The passing of time only makes the moments more precious.

As we entered my Uncle Vladimir's house, the sweet scent of evergreen filled our nostrils from the Tree that lay on the parlor floor.

"The Christmas Tree!" my brother, my two cousins and I chirped.

"Indeed it is," Aunt Svetlana and Uncle Vladimir said as they both hugged and kissed us all.

We children called my Uncle Vladimir "Vova." A small name for such a big and gentle man, and although he was quite old, Christmas was a time that made him young again.

The wise Icon seemed to look back at me from the corner of the parlor. Sheaves of wheat stood in a small bundle on the little table under it.

"For a good harvest and so this house will never know hunger," Uncle Vova said.

The kitchen was filled with glorious aromas of wonderful things that were being prepared for the coming feast later that day. My grandma and aunties were each making their own *kutya,* a thick porridge of wheat or rice with honey, poppyseeds, raisins and nuts. The aunties each came from a different part of Russia so each of their recipes was different.

"They are all delicious," my grandpa would say, trying to keep peace.

Later, we watched Uncle Vova and Aunt Svetlana dance around the brightly wrapped packages. He loved to dance with her and tell her how beautiful she was. "I am so lucky to have stolen your heart so many years ago," he'd say. She would blush and say, "Oh Volodya." Then she'd giggle.

After the dancing, he looked at his watch and said, "Isn't it time to be making paper stars?" We raced to the kitchen table to make our stars out of colored paper. I got to hold the one that Uncle Vova made.

While we were busy making our stars in the kitchen, my Grandma Carle went into the parlor and closed the big double doors. There, she decorated the Christmas tree in secret. She lovingly took each ornament and hung it on the tree. She became a child again by remembering something warm about each and every one. Small bells rang softly, hearts danced about merrily, painted *pysanky* eggs graced the branches.

When she finished she smiled deeply, sighed, then slipped through the parlor doors and closed them so that we could not see the tree until after dinner.

Uncle Vova had been watching us make our stars. When we were done, we looked at him with anticipation. He knew what we were waiting for him to say, but he teased us and made us wait ever so long.

Finally, with a grand gesture he took his watch from his pocket and announced, "Could it be time to take our paper stars..." Then he paused and teased us even more, "...out...for a...sleighride?!"

"Yipppppeeeeeeeeeeeeeee," we all squealed! That was what we were waiting to hear. We raced to pull on our heavy wool coats, boots and mufflers.

Grandpa had been heating soap stones in the stove. He wrapped them in old wool blankets and took them out to the sleigh and put them on the floor under burlap bags to keep us warm.

We all marched up the hill with our stars. Squeak...squeak...squeak went our boots in the snow. Up the hill we went to where grandpa held the sleigh.

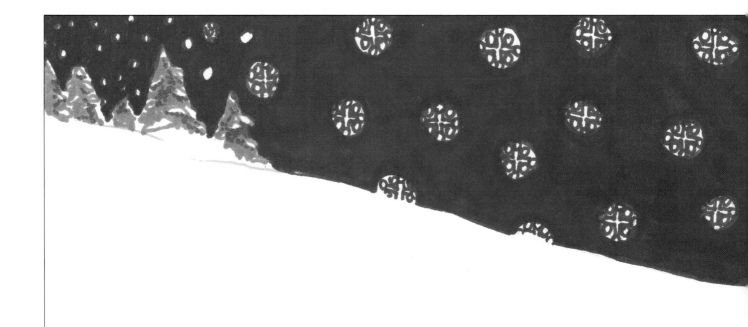

Uncle Vova clicked and gently tugged the reins, and the sleigh swooshed smoothly down the hill. Billows of steam came out of the horse's nostrils with a soft puffing sound, and his hooves made a muffled clip, clop, clop as they met the new snow.

We all sang songs...wonderful songs that echoed off the bark of the evergreens as we passed them.

"I wonder what the dinner table will look like?" my cousins mused out loud. My thoughts trailed off back to the farmhouse.

I knew that while we were gone, Grandma, Aunt Svetlana and Aunt Ykaterina were busy laying the table for dinner. First with straw and hay to remember and honor the stable in Bethlehem. Over the straw, they would put a glistening white linen table cloth and their best silver and finest china.

On the sideboard would be cakes shaped like cupolas, and rum babba, hard candies and taffy. The dining room table would be transformed from that of a midwestern farmhouse into a shimmering festival table deep in the heartland of Russia.

As the sleigh finally drew into the driveway of the farmhouse, we circled the tall evergreen tree that stood in the middle of the driveway loop.

"When Svetlana and I arrived from our homeland, we planted this tree together to celebrate our own "roots" being put down into the new land," Uncle Vova said, as we got out of the sleigh. We all went to the barn to get strings of berries and popcorn to put on the tree. We also hung small bags of sewet and grain for the wild birds.

"For you," Uncle Vova said to the birds.

The final touch was to hang the paper stars we had made on the branches.

"Always remember to do this at Christmas, my darlings...even when
I'm gone," Uncle Vova said quietly, as the animals went to the tree.

"Volodya," Aunt Svetlana called out from the kitchen window. "You come now for dinner!"

We all ran into the house to wash for dinner.

Kutya was served from a giant turine in the center of the table. Before we ate, Uncle Vova filled a bowl for those of the family who were no longer there.

"We remember," he said softly.

Then he flung a spoonful of *kutya* onto the ceiling. The number of grains of rice that stuck there prophesied the number of bees we could expect in the spring. This annoyed Aunt Svetlana, but she ended up laughing with the rest of us.

Another spoonful was flung out the window. "For Grandfather Frost," Uncle Vova said. "Here is a spoonful for thee. Please do not touch our crops!" Then he said a blessing and the feast began.

We children ate the *kutya* so fast we almost choked. We were anxious to get to the bottom of the bowl, for in one of them was a new silver dollar. Whoever got it had the best luck ever!

"Here it is," my brother's voice crowed. The rest of the feast was eaten more slowly and with great pleasure.

When dinner was finished, Uncle Vova looked at the clock, then waited. He watched us lean forward in our seats, ready to burst with excitement. A mere nod from him meant we could open the parlor doors.

"Could it be that time already?" he started to say. Then he paused for the longest time. Finally he winked and nodded. We bolted from our seats and leaped toward the parlor.

The first sight of the tree took our breath away.

It shimmered with light of its own. Candles glowed on its branches. Small toys beckoned our touch, sugarplums and candied ginger invited us to taste. The tree was resplendent with *pysanky* eggs, peppermint hearts and small ringing bells.

Our eyes must have sparkled, for Uncle Vova took such pleasure in watching us. His merry eyes danced and twinkled as he heard each child scream and gasp with excitement as we opened our gifts.

"Such joy...such magic," he sighed as he leaned back in his old, worn, easy chair.

This was to be a bittersweet memory, for that was the last Christmas Uncle Vova was with us.

At the next Christmas dinner a bowl of *kutya* was placed in Uncle Vova's empty place. We all softly murmured, "We remember."

"He would have wanted us to keep Christmas as always," Grandma said sadly.

"He would have wanted this house to be filled with laughter and good cheer," Aunt Svetlana said softly.

"But it is so hard without him," Grandpa said.

Suddenly, my brother jumped out of his seat and hollered. "The tree!... THE TREEEEEEE!" he screeched, "We forgot to decorate Uncle Vova's tree."

My brother, my cousins and I started to pull on our overcoats and race outside to decorate the tree.

"Look!" Aunt Svetlana called out as she pointed out the window. We all stood, stunned at what we saw. "A miracle," Ykaterina whispered.

Not a sleigh's length from us the animals were dressing Uncle Vova's tree. The birds were bringing berries and dropping them onto the snow-filled boughs...geese, ducks, chickens, goats and lambs moved silently toward the tree as if called there by an unheard voice. They were joined by wild animals from the forest nearby.

There in the moonlight, with the stars flashing like diamonds, the tree shimmered in its own glowing light. It looked miraculous and wonderful.

"He is here," I said. "I can feel Uncle Vova here, now."

This was a Christmas that blazes in my memory, for in the midst of our despair, we had felt only love with its center in Uncle Vova's tree.